Gramps' Favorite Gift

by Tanisha Carr
illustrated by Craig Orback

 HOUGHTON MIFFLIN   BOSTON

Printed in China

ISBN-13: 978-0-547-01877-5
ISBN-10: 0-547-01877-0

15 16 17 18 0940 19 18 17 16
4500569761

Quentin hopped off the bus, carrying his math homework in one hand and the saxophone that his mother had asked him to bring home in the other. He wasn't sure what he dreaded more, the homework or his mother's special "assignment."

Quentin loved playing saxophone in the school band. The songs came so easily to him that he rarely had to practice outside of the band studio.

But now his mother wanted him to play some old jazz songs from the 1940s, and he wasn't interested at all. The songs sounded nothing like the popular songs that he listened to on the radio.

Marcus climbed off the bus next, clutching his "Top Secret" notebook. He was Quentin's older brother and a model student. He always put a lot of effort into his work and always finished his assignments on time, sometimes even early!

His notebook held all of the song lyrics and poems that he'd written. Very few people had ever seen them, and no one had heard them, except for Marcus himself. Unlike his brother, he liked music that was calmer and more meaningful. He was too shy to sing, but he could hear how the songs would sound in his mind. He'd been taking piano lessons since first grade, so he knew how to write out the music notes, too.

Marcus wanted to play the keyboard in a band someday when he was older. He'd find someone with a great voice to sing his words and he would lead the band from the background.

As the brothers walked home, they were both thinking about their conversation at dinner the night before. Their mother had shared her plans for their grandfather's 80th birthday party. She'd waited until the boys were eating their favorite dessert, banana pudding, to reveal how they were going to be involved. She wanted them to learn to play their grandfather's favorite songs from his college days. Neither of them looked very happy when she shared her plans.

"He'll be so excited to hear them again. And he'll be so proud that you learned them, too!" she'd told them excitedly. "Why don't we listen to a couple of the songs now," she had added, walking to the stereo. The two brothers had looked pleadingly at their father for help. He'd just smiled and continued to eat his dessert. They knew that this wasn't a request.

The songs sounded
old-fashioned and odd.
The horns and piano were
all over the place and Quentin
couldn't tell one song from the
next. Marcus understood the music
a little better, but it wasn't his style.

"This is going to make your grandfather
so happy!" their mother had said with a big smile as
she handed them the written sheet music. "I was able
to get these from the music store downtown. Do you
think two songs will be enough?" she'd asked.

"Yes, Mother!" they'd answered together, the
sound of dread clear in their voices.

Now, as the brothers approached their house, Quentin finally brought up their mother's assignment.

"I don't even like jazz," he moaned. "And why did she have to pick such hard songs for us to learn?"

Marcus was a little less concerned. "That's just what Gramps liked when he was young like us."

"You might need to help me out. It all sounds the same to me," Quentin said.

"Okay. Let's get started after dinner. The schedule is pretty tough. I can't believe Mom only gave us two weeks to learn both these songs."

Marcus spent some time that afternoon looking up information about jazz on the Internet. If he was going to play it, he wanted to understand it. He learned that certain parts of the music are written down, or composed, so that they can be learned and repeated by other musicians. Other parts are made up as the song goes along.

When the brothers met at the piano later, Marcus told Quentin how the jazz songs were written. "I'll play the basic written parts, and you can play whatever sounds right to you," he explained. "You can work out some solo ideas to feature the saxophone, or you can just make it up as you go."

"But where do I start?" Quentin asked, feeling doubtful. "This music streaks by so quickly."

"We'll practice the parts slowly to begin with," Marcus answered.

The songs sounded rough the first few times they played them. Quentin was starting to get tired and frustrated by hearing all their mistakes, so he made a suggestion. "Let's listen to the record again."

"Good idea," Marcus replied. "And I already downloaded it onto my laptop. We can listen here."

"Now, that was a good idea," Quentin complimented his brother. As the boys listened, Quentin began to move his fingers along with some difficult sections. He noticed that Marcus hummed along with the music, too. That was unusual, because Marcus was often too shy about his voice to sing or hum.

"Let's play along this time. I think I'm starting to understand enough to really appreciate the song."

After the song ended, Quentin said, "Now I see what happens in that section I ruined before. The rhythm changes."

"Yeah, you're right," his brother replied. "The drummer sort of yanked the whole band back on its heels. Then they all fell right back into the original beat together."

"That must have been tough for such a big band!" Quentin said. He was clearly impressed.

While the boys were practicing, their parents were washing the dishes at the other end of the house. "They sound as if they're gaining a little respect for this old jazz music," their father said to their mom.

"Well, that was half of my plan, wasn't it?" she winked, passing him a soapy plate.

The days passed quickly. As the songs came together, the boys found that they looked forward to playing them. Before long, it was time for their grandfather's birthday party. The house was packed with friends and family. Everyone brought presents and food. This party was a feast, packed with tables of tasty treats.

In the center of the room, Gramps sat in a big lounge chair. He reached up to hug each of his children and grandchildren as they arrived. Though he couldn't walk very well, he seemed full of energy, clearly touched by all of the people who had come.

Before long, it was time for dinner. Everyone stood in a circle holding hands and Gramps thanked them all for coming. His eyes welled up as he told everyone how touched he was to see his whole family together in the same room. "And doesn't this meal look absolutely glorious," he said, licking his lips.

While everyone was so busy celebrating, one little toddler leaned across the table for the birthday cake. She grabbed a mouthful and smeared icing all over her face. Everyone laughed, although her mother didn't seem too happy.

The family lined up for the buffet, and after someone brought Gramps a plate, the line began to move. As Marcus waited, he began to feel more nervous than he had expected. The first plate of food made him feel better, so he went back for seconds.

Quentin never liked to play the sax with a stomach full of food, so he only ate a little bit. But he did have a weakness for sweets, so he piled several cookies and pieces of cake on a platter to sample after the music!

After the dishes were cleared, their mother cleared her throat to get everyone's attention. "Now, Papa, before you open your gifts, Marcus and Quentin have a special treat for you," she announced.

The two brothers each took a deep breath and nodded at the other. Quentin snapped his fingers a couple of times to establish the beat, and then Marcus's hands began to fly over the piano keys.

Their grandfather's face lit up into a knowing smile. He recognized the tune right away.

After a few moments, Quentin closed his eyes and began to breathe life into his saxophone.

Before long, toes were tapping and fingers were snapping throughout the room. Gramps danced along to the beat in his chair.

Sometimes Quentin played along with the piano, and other times he played *against* its beat. Marcus listened carefully, and he responded by changing his piano playing. The music was like a beautiful conversation between the two brothers.

At one point, Quentin surprised his brother—and everyone else—by blowing a phrase from "Happy Birthday" on his saxophone. Everyone cheered. Then Marcus seamlessly fit lines from a popular song into the tune they were playing. The room erupted again. The two boys were really playing jazz.

As their mother had predicted, Quentin and Marcus's performance was their grandfather's favorite gift that year.

Responding

✓ TARGET SKILL **Understanding Characters**

How do Quentin's thoughts, actions, and words show his attitude before the performance in *Gramps' Favorite Gift*? Copy and complete the chart below.

Thoughts	Actions	Words
Quentin isn't at all interested in playing jazz for his grandfather.	?	?

Write About It

Text to Self Think of a time when you were asked to try something new. Write a paragraph in which you describe how you felt at first and then describe how you felt afterward.

✔ TARGET VOCABULARY

concerned	schedule
feast	smeared
glorious	streak
model	studio
ruined	yanked

✔ **TARGET SKILL** **Understanding Characters** Use details to tell more about characters.

✔ **TARGET STRATEGY** **Visualize** Use text details to form pictures in your mind of what you are reading.

GENRE **Realistic Fiction** is a present-day story that could take place in real life.